LOST
IN THE SWAMP OF TERROR

TRACEY TURNER

Crabtree Publishing Company
www.crabtreebooks.com

Crabtree Publishing Company
www.crabtreebooks.com
1-800-387-7650

616 Welland Ave.
St. Catharines, ON
L2M 5V6

PMB 59051, 350 Fifth Ave.
59th Floor,
New York, NY

Published by Crabtree Publishing Company in 2016.

Author: Tracey Turner

Illustrator: Nelson Evergreen

Editorial Director: Kathy Middleton

Editor: Petrice Custance

Proofreader: Janine Deschenes

Prepress technician: Tammy McGarr

Print and Production coordinator: Katherine Berti

WARNING!

The instructions in this book are for extreme survival situations only. Always proceed with caution, and ask an adult to supervise—or, if possible, seek expert help. If in doubt, consult a responsible adult.

First published 2016 by A & C Black, an imprint of Bloomsbury Publishing Plc.

Printed in Canada/032016/EF20160210

Library and Archives Canada Cataloguing in Publication

Turner, Tracey, author
Lost in the swamp of terror / Tracey Turner.

(Lost : can you survive?)
Includes index.
ISBN 978-0-7787-2354-7 (bound).--ISBN 978-0-7787-2356-1 (paperback)

1. Plot-your-own stories. I. Title.

PZ7.T883Lostin 2016 j823′.92 C2015-907486-X

Library of Congress Cataloging-in-Publication Data

CIP available at the Library of Congress

Contents

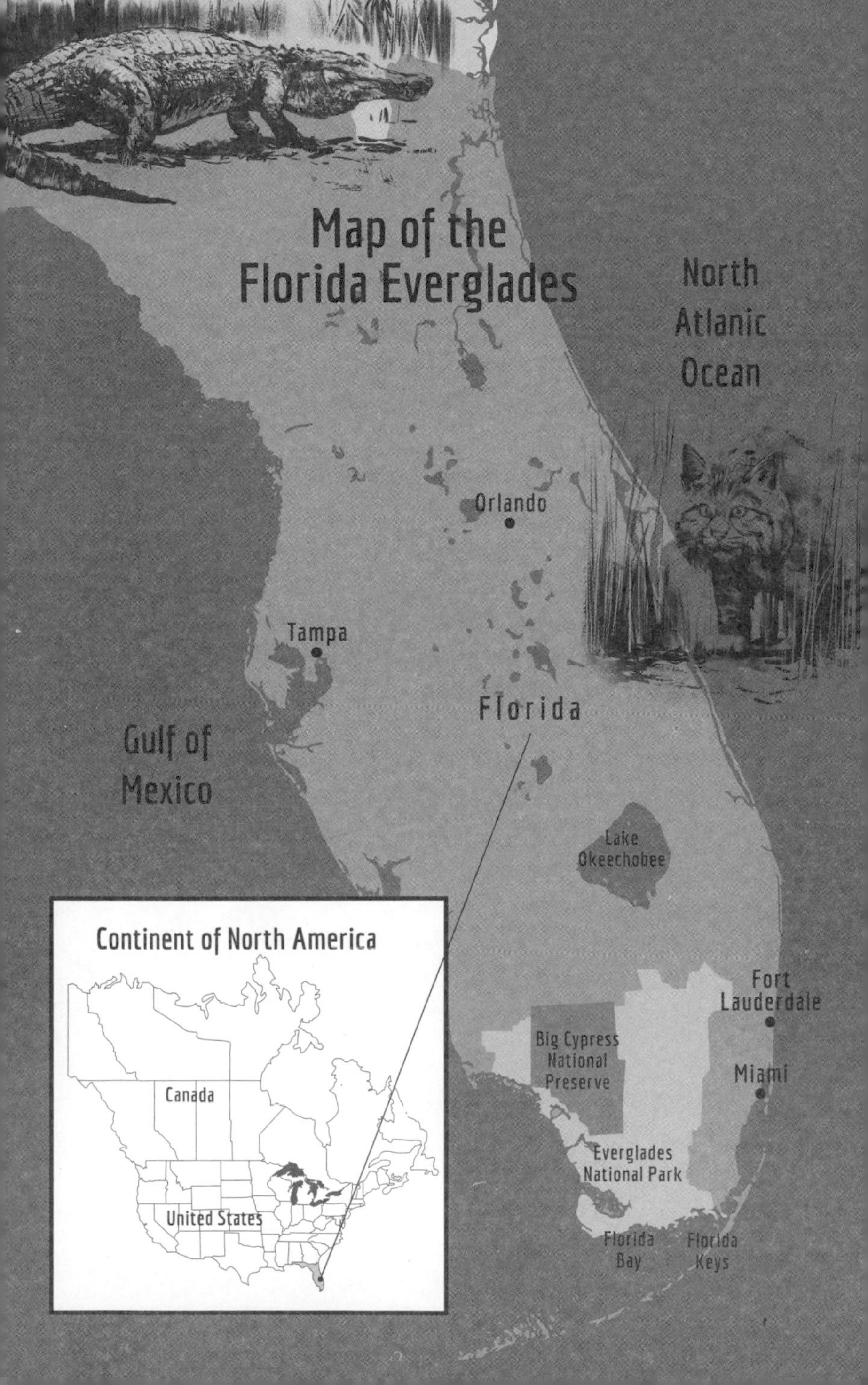
Map of the Florida Everglades
North Atlantic Ocean
Orlando
Tampa
Florida
Gulf of Mexico
Lake Okeechobee
Continent of North America
Canada
United States
Fort Lauderdale
Big Cypress National Preserve
Miami
Everglades National Park
Florida Bay
Florida Keys

Welcome to your Adventure!

STOP! Read this first!

Welcome to an action-packed adventure in which you take the starring role!

You're about to enter the Everglades in Florida, USA—a wild land of forest, flooded grassland, and alligator-infested swamps. On each page, choose from the different options—according to your instincts, knowledge, and intelligence—and make your own path through the wilderness to safety.

You decide...

- How to escape a stalking panther
- How to navigate a mangrove swamp
- How to tell a harmless snake from a deadly one

...and many more life-or-death dilemmas. Along the way you'll discover the facts you need to help you survive.

It's time to test your survival skills—or die trying!

Your adventure starts on page 7.

You open your eyes blearily. You're slumped against a tree trunk. A sharp pain on your forehead reminds you that you hit your head when you accidentally walked into a branch. You must have been knocked unconscious.

You stand up and look around. You're in the middle of what looks like a primeval swamp. Trees draped in moss stand in murky brown water that reaches to your ankles. The croaks of frogs, calls of birds, and the buzz of insects fill the humid air. You jump backwards with a splash as something slithers past your foot in the dark water below.

You came to the Everglades as part of a guided group on a wilderness tour, far away from the well-trodden tourist tracks. You got here at dawn. You have no idea how long you've been unconscious, but you think it still looks like morning. Your group is nowhere to be seen. You didn't know anyone else on the tour. Maybe they haven't even noticed you're missing.

You have no idea how to find your way back to civilization. You are completely lost and alone in this swampy wilderness.

With only the croaks of frogs for company, you tighten the straps on your backpack and set off.

How will you survive?

Turn to page 8 to find information you need to help you survive.

You are lost in the Everglades in Florida, USA. When you think of Florida, you might picture theme parks, big cities, and beaches crowded with countless sunbathers. But the southern part of the state is a wet, mosquito-ridden wilderness, where alligators and venomous snakes lurk. People have walked into the Everglades never to return.

River of Grass

Most of the state of Florida is a peninsula, a huge finger of land that points into the sea. In the middle of Florida, Lake Okeechobee drains down to the sea in the rainy season (which is the summer time in Florida). South of the lake, the land is made of limestone rock that slopes gently down to the sea. So the southern part of Florida—including what's now the Everglades—is really a very slow-moving river, as the large lake drains into Florida Bay, flooding grasslands and forests on its way, with the water level rising and falling from season to season. For this reason, the Everglades area is sometimes known as the River of Grass. Some of the land has been reclaimed and used as farmland or to build towns, cities, and roads. But the southern tip of the Florida peninsula, surrounded by the sea, remains the wet wilderness it's been for thousands of years.

Patchwork Habitats

The Everglades is a patchwork of different habitats. Lower ground forms "sloughs," which are like rivers flowing through the grassland, and are wet all year round, even when the grassland is almost dry. On higher ground, there are forests of hardwood trees known as hammocks, and rocky pinewoods. Clumps of cypress trees, with their bases always underwater, form swampy forests. Mangrove swamps line the coast, gradually giving way to the ocean. Each of these different habitats is home to a unique collection of plants and animals. You will encounter all of them on your adventure—if you make it to the end.

Deadly Danger

The dangers that might await you in the Everglades include alligators, crocodiles, deadly snakes and spiders, snapping turtles, sharks, biting insects, poisonous plants, and tropical storms. The terrain can be dangerous, too, with deep sinkholes opening up in the rock where you least expect to find them, and thick, sucking mud.

Turn to page 10.

Surviving the Swamp

- It's November, which is at the beginning of the dry season so you should see cooler temperatures than the summer months. However, for your visit it's still hot and humid, and water levels are quite high.
- You're wearing lightweight clothing that covers your arms and legs, and walking boots, which are completely saturated.
- You have plenty of insect-repellent. Florida is famous for mosquitoes and other biting insects.
- Drinkable water is hard to find, since the water moves so slowly (or not at all). You have several full bottles of drinking water in your backpack. It won't be enough to keep you hydrated, but will keep you going for a couple of days.
- There are animals in the Everglades that can easily kill you. Approach animals with caution, even if you don't think they're dangerous. And always keep your distance.
- A predator is more likely to see you as prey and chase you if you're running away from it.
- Panic is your enemy. You are in a dangerous place, but you need a clear head to enable you to make good decisions and survive. But you need luck on your side as well.

Turn to page 11.

You call out in case the rest of your group is still close by. You strain your ears for any sound that might mean humans. A bird screeches loudly from the tree canopy...and a distant low bellow sends a shiver down your spine. All around you are the sounds of drips and splashes in this watery world. But there's nothing to give you hope that people might be nearby.

The muddy ground is under a bit of water, and you squelch along. The air feels heavy with moisture, and it's hot, which makes walking hard work. You jump in alarm as a water snake darts out from under your foot. You quickly grab a fallen branch to use as a walking stick, and to warn small creatures to move away. What if you stepped on a venomous snake by accident?

Go to page 12.

Your heart is pounding, but you pull yourself together and try to think clearly. You need to figure out which way your group might have headed.

The plan was that the day's tour would end with canoeing in the mangroves. Do you think the mangroves are to the south? Or to the east? The sun is behind a cloud, but you can just about make out where it is. How can you use it to tell you which way to go?

If you decide to walk with the sun to your left, go to page 18.

If you decide to walk in the direction of the sun, go to page 25.

Everglades Cypress Dome Habitat

- You're in the middle of a cypress dome—a swampy forest of (mainly) pond cypress trees, which grow with their bases in water.
- The trees form a dome, which you can see from a distance, though not when you're amongst the trees. Taller trees grow in the center because the soil is richer there. The land in the center of the dome is lower than the sides, but even so the tops of the trees there are higher than the ones further away from the center.
- In cypress domes, the waterline rises and falls seasonally—the wet season is in summer—but the bases of the trees are almost always in water, especially in the center.
- All kinds of plants live in cypress domes, including rare orchids. The trees are hung with Spanish moss, which looks like trailing green beards. Spiky air-breathing plants cling to them. Some of these plants are members of the same family as pineapples, and some have brightly colored flowers.
- All sorts of creatures lurk in cypress forest habitats, including the highly venomous cottonmouth snake, water snakes, turtles, and of course the alligators that thrive in the watery environment of the Everglades.

The alligator doesn't seem bothered by your presence. But as you get closer, you hear a strange hissing noise. You soon realize that it's coming from the alligator.

Maybe you should turn around and run away from it after all?

If you decide to get away from the alligator, go to page 20.

If you choose to carry on past it, go to page 26.

You're glad you changed direction. It's much e to walk with the water lapping at your ankles rather than over your knees, and you feel less anxious about large animals lurking unseen in the murky water. (If you want to find out about a creature with a very powerful bite, turn to page 31.)

You hear some splashing ahead of you and peer through the trees. You can't see what's making the noise. You wonder briefly if you should walk in a different direction, but everywhere around you looks equally inhospitable.

Go to page 18.

The water isn't as high here and you can see the tops of your boots for the first time in a while. As you carry on walking, you notice that the water has almost disappeared. You're now squelching through thick, sucking mud. It's not easy.

Ahead of you, the gloom of the trees seems to be getting lighter. You think you can see a way out of this swampy cypress forest. You swat away yet another mosquito and walk on.

Go to page 38.

The way ahead looks darker and wetter than ever. Thin, knobbly tree stumps stick up out of the water. These are called cypress knees, and they're actually cypress tree roots that stick up out of the water.

Although you sometimes find yourself entangled in underwater roots, the cypress knees are useful as hand-holds. Even so, it's difficult to walk through it. Maybe it would be better to choose a different route and try to find a way out of this jungle environment?

If you decide to carry on, go to page 32.

If you decide to try and find a way out, go to page 55.

A loud splash makes you turn around. What you see makes your heart pound violently: a huge alligator is chasing a turtle! The alligator makes a sudden lunge forward and snaps its powerful jaws. The turtle just manages to escape, slipping down into the water and away from the hungry alligator.

The alligator has missed its breakfast.

Earlier this morning—though it seems like a very long time ago now—the guide told your group that alligators very rarely attack people. He said that when he has come across one, he just pushed it firmly so that it moved away, and not one alligator has ever snapped at him. If your guide is to be believed, then maybe you shouldn't be bothered by this animal. Although it does look very big.

If you decide to give the alligator a safe distance, go to page 36.

If you decide not to worry too much about the alligator, go to page 14.

Everglades Turtles

- There are many different kinds of turtles living in the Everglades. The one you've just seen is a Florida softshell turtle, a favourite food for alligators.
- As their name suggests, they don't have the hard protective shell that other turtles do. Their shell is leathery on top and soft at the edges. To compensate for this weak armour, softshell turtles are fast movers. They have long thin noses, like mini trunks, which they use as snorkels.
- Other turtles found in the Everglades include box turtles, terrapins, and snapping turtles.
- In the coastal waters of the Everglades, there are five different species of sea turtle, all of which are endangered or threatened. They include green turtles, leatherbacks, loggerheads, hawksbills, and Kemp's ridley.

You were right to get away. Alligators make that hissing sound as a warning, and it was a very big and hungry alligator.

You're wondering what else might be lurking here when you spot something that makes your heart skip a beat: coiled in a patch of sunlight is an enormous, thick snake with patterned brown and green skin. Thankfully it's about 10 feet (3 m) away, and shows no sign of having seen you. You quicken your steps, shuddering.

Perhaps you should find a way out of this swampy forest? You think you can see more light over to your right. Maybe it's a way out? On the other hand, everywhere in the Everglades is completely outside your experience, and there could be dangerous animals anywhere.

If you decide to try and find a way out, go to page 38.

If you decide to keep going, go to page 54.

Snakes of the Everglades

- The snake you've just seen is a boa constrictor, which can measure nearly 13.1 feet (4 m) long. These snakes constrict their prey by squeezing them to death rather than injecting them with venom. Boas are not native to the Everglades, but come from Central and South America. And they're not the only constricting invaders . . .

- Burmese pythons are a well-known problem in the Everglades. The species is native to southeast Asia, but was introduced here when (probably) pet snakes escaped or were set free when they became big and dangerous. There are now thousands of them. (Turn to page 101 for more information on Burmese pythons.)

- Most snakes in the Everglades are not venomous. These include the Eastern indigo snake, which, at up to 9 feet (2.75 m) long, is the longest native snake in the United States. Corn snakes, rat snakes, and various different water snakes are also harmless.

- There are venomous snakes in the Everglades. Rattlesnakes, eastern coral snakes, and cottonmouths (see pages 53, 45, and 23) all live here.

The flooded forest floor and tangle of tree roots makes it difficult to move. You reach out and grab another of the cypress knees to help you. Unfortunately, you disturb a snake. Alarmed, it strikes at you and bites your hand.

It's true that there are more non-venomous snakes in the Everglades than there are venomous ones, but that doesn't mean there aren't plenty of dangerous snakes here. This one is a highly venomous cottonmouth. Its bite delivers a fatal injection into your bloodstream.

The bite is painful and your hand quickly becomes bruised and sore. You start to feel weak and out of breath, and you slump down to rest on a tree stump. You don't get up again.

The end.

Cottonmouths

- Cottonmouths, also known as water moccasins, live both on land and in the water. They've even been known to swim in the sea. They're found in the southeastern United States.
- Cottonmouths are a type of pit viper. They have two heat-sensitive pits between their eyes and nostrils that can detect prey.
- They are big snakes, and can grow to be more than 3.3 feet (1 m) long.
- Cottonmouths' colors and patterns vary. Most adults are black or almost black, while some keep part of the banded pattern they have as youngsters. Young cottonmouths are often brightly colored.
- The name "cottonmouth" is a reference to the inside of the snake's mouth, which is white in color (like cotton). If the snake feels threatened, it often opens its mouth to reveal its fangs.
- Cottonmouths' venom can kill people.

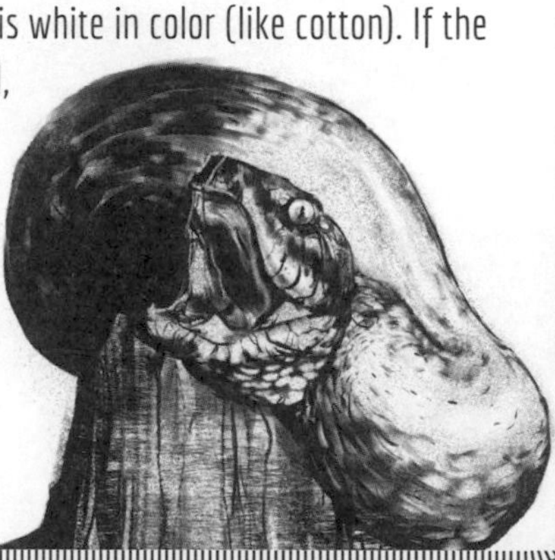

You're tired, but you tell yourself that you can't afford to stop and rest. The most important thing is to find rescue. You think that, surely, people must be looking for you by now.

Although it's still hot and humid, and the ground is damp, it feels good to be on dry land and not wading through water. Suddenly you hear an unfamiliar sound, like someone shaking a maraca. You pause and look around. You can't see anything unusual. Perhaps it's a cricket of some kind—they make all sorts of weird noises. But maybe you should retrace your steps, and head in a different direction?

If you decide to go a different way, go to page 80.

If you decide to carry on, go to page 48.

The water starts to become deeper, and it's now lapping around your knees.

Should you carry on anyway, or change direction and find shallower water?

If you decide to find shallower water, go to page 15.

If you decide to carry on, go to page 30.

It's true that alligators rarely attack people in the Everglades. However, this one is very big, and very hungry—and it's just missed out on a meal.

The hissing noise is the alligator warning you to back off. When you don't, it covers the distance between you surprisingly quickly and attacks.

The alligator's powerful jaws snap around you, and the animal rolls over and over in the water to drown you. This is known as a "death roll." It's all over very quickly.

The end.

American Alligator

- American alligators live in the southeastern United States (mainly Florida and Louisiana), in freshwater swamps, rivers, and lakes.
- Alligators can measure up to 14.8 feet (4.5 m) long, though adults are about 9.8 feet (3 m) long on average. They can weigh up to about 992 pounds (450 kg)
- Alligators prey mainly on fish, turtles, snakes, and small mammals. They're not fussy, though, and will try and eat whatever comes their way if they're hungry.
- Large alligators do attack people, but there have been fewer than 30 recorded deaths in the last 70 years.
- American alligators were once hunted for their skins, and were nearly wiped out. They've made a successful comeback, and today they're not endangered.

Walking across the flooded grassland is nowhere near as easy as you thought it would be. Underneath the water, the rock can be sharp, and the mud is slippery. But worst of all is the grass itself. It has serrated edges that tear at your clothes, and make nasty cuts in your skin.

You look down to where the grass has ripped your trousers. The exposed skin on your legs is now covered in cuts from the grass. You've got insect bites all over your arms and legs, and you are trying hard not to scratch them.

Should you change plan and walk toward the pine trees after all?

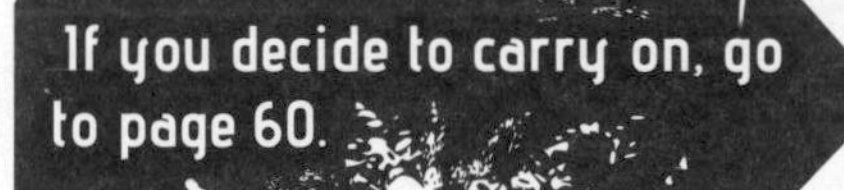
If you decide to carry on, go to page 60.

If you decide to make for the pine trees, go to page 49.

Sawgrass

- The grass here, known as sawgrass, is actually a type of plant called sedge. It grows on a mud and limestone base called "marl."

- If you look very carefully at the sawgrass leaves, you'll see that they have sharp, serrated edges that can cut skin and clothes.

- Sawgrass used to grow further north in the Everglades, in an area that has now been reclaimed for growing sugarcane. In the richer soil there, sawgrass would reach more than 9.8 feet (3 m) tall.

- Sawgrass marshes here are flooded for between six and twelve months of the year. How tall and thick the plant grows depends on how much of the year it's been flooded. The more time it spends underwater, the thicker and taller it grows.

- Other plants grow amongst the sawgrass, including carnivorous plants such as bladderwort, which traps insects.

You walk through the increasingly deep water, which is now up to your waist. You're thinking about turning back when suddenly you feel a terrible pain in your hand. You pull it out of the water and see that it's pouring with blood! Something has bitten you!

You have been very unlucky. An alligator snapping turtle was lurking unseen beneath the water, waiting for a fish or another small creature to come along. Unfortunately, it mistook your fingers for its prey. Its powerful jaws can easily bite through flesh and bone.

Your injury wouldn't be enough to kill you if you weren't lost, tired, and very far from a hospital or any kind of help at all. However, alone and without any medical attention, you soon lose consciousness from blood loss, and don't wake up again.

The end.

Alligator Snapping Turtle

- Alligator snapping turtles live in the southeastern United States. They're the largest freshwater turtle in North America. Their shells can measure up to about 27.6 inches (70 cm) in length.

- The turtles entice their prey by using their tongues as a bait. They lay about with their mouths open and their tongues wiggling, hoping that fish will mistake their tongue for a worm.

- These turtles look very strange. Their shells are steeply ridged (a bit like the ridges on an alligator's back), and their jaws look like beaks. As you've just found out, these jaws are extremely powerful.

- Florida snapping turtles also live in the Everglades. They are much smaller than alligator snapping turtles, don't have ridges on their backs, and aren't nearly as ugly. They can still bite off a finger though!

You reach out to grasp a cypress knee, but pull your hand away in fright as a snake slithers off it and into the water.

There are snakes here but your guide said that the vast majority are harmless. All the same, maybe you should go back?

If you decide to carry on, go to page 22.

If you decide to go back, go to page 55.

You take off your soaking shoes and socks. They won't dry out in this humidity, but it's still good to have some air on your feet.

You settle down to have a rest underneath some plants that look like mini palm trees, with spiky leaves. These are saw palmetto, and they are very common here in the pine forest. You have to be careful of the leaves though, because they have serrated edges that can cut. However, lying beneath them in the shade, you're quite comfortable. You notice cobwebs on the undersides of the leaves as you lie down for a rest.

You make yourself comfortable and close your eyes.

Go to page 62.

The dolphins keep coming back to your canoe, jumping and splashing around it. You know that dolphins enjoy playing in the wake of a fast-moving boat, but who knows why they're interested in you. Maybe they're just curious.

The dolphins swim away, and as you watch them go you spot what might have frightened them off: the large, dark shape of a shark. Its fin slices through the water, like a scene from your worst nightmares. After a few tense moments you realize, with relief, that it isn't interested in you, and you watch it swim away.

You're scanning the sea for other dangers when you spot a much more welcome sight: there's a motor boat heading your way! You paddle towards it, stopping to wave every few minutes.

Go to page 114.

Sharks of Florida Bay

There is a huge variety of marine life in Florida Bay, including sharks.

- Blacktip sharks are fairly small. The biggest are less than 6.6 feet (2 m) long. Even so, they've been known to attack people.
- Great hammerhead sharks use their hammer-shaped heads to detect prey over a wide area. Their eyes are widely spaced, and special organs that detect other animals are also spread out across their wide heads. Their favorite prey are stingrays. These sharks are big, measuring up to about 18 feet (5.5 m) long, and are dangerous to humans.
- Nurse sharks are usually found near the sea bed. They use Florida Bay's mangrove islands as nurseries for baby sharks.
- Tiger sharks, measuring up to about 18 feet (5.5 m) long, are some of the most dangerous sharks to humans, along with great white sharks and bull sharks (see page 85).

You move away from the alligator, but keep your eye on the enormous creature. You don't want to be anywhere near something that big and hungry. You hope it doesn't dive under the water, where you won't be able to tell where it is. Luckily, the alligator doesn't move.

You're feeling a bit better now that there's a good distance between you and the huge creature.

Suddenly you're plunged into water that reaches up to your neck! The shock makes you cry out. You've just discovered one of the many sinkholes in the limestone rock here. It's not very big or deep, but it gave you a nasty shock.

You scramble out the other side, and come face to face with a curious, furry face, with dark patches over its eyes. You recognize it as a raccoon, one of the mammals that makes the Everglades their home. It scampers off as you climb out of the sinkhole.

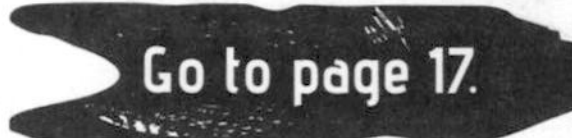
Go to page 17.

Mammals of the Everglades

Around 40 different mammal species live in the Everglades. Here are just a few of them:

- Raccoons live throughout most of North America, in all sorts of habitats—marshes, forests, prairies, towns, and cities. They'll eat just about anything. They can open garbage bins, which is partly why they're in no danger of extinction.

- Marsh rabbits are another common Everglades mammal. They have shorter ears than most other kinds of rabbit, and can swim short distances.

- You might spot a gray fox in a hardwood hammock. They're the only foxes in the world that can climb trees.

- White-tailed deer, found all over the eastern United States, are also found here (see page 103). Deer in the Everglades tend to be smaller than deer in other parts of the world because Florida's warmer temperatures mean they don't need extra fat.

- Everglades mammals are threatened by the constricting snakes that have been introduced to Florida (see pages 21 and 101).

It's not long before you reach the edge of the forest. Flooded grassland stretches into the distance. Not far away, there's a pine tree forest on higher ground, which looks dry.

Should you make for the pine forest? It might be better to be on dry land for a change. Or should you head southwards, towards the coast? Maybe it's better to be out in the open, even if it means wading through the flooded grassland.

If you decide to walk across the flooded grassland southward, go to page 28.

If you decide to make for the pine forest, go to page 50.

Sawgrass Marsh Habitat

- Sawgrass marsh looks like flooded grassland, and is probably the kind of landscape that comes to mind when you think of the Everglades. It stays wet for most of the year, but in the dry season it begins to dry out and you can see the ground.

- You might spot floating periphyton amongst the sawgrass. These are spongy, wet clumps of algae. The periphyton forms the bottom of the food chain, and small water creatures feed on it. In turn, they are eaten by bigger creatures, and so on up to large predators.

- Alligators lurk in sawgrass marshes. You might also find turtles here, as well as marsh rabbits and white-tailed deer.

- Within sawgrass marshes there are deeper areas known as sloughs (pronounced "slews") which stay wet even in the dry season. In the Everglades there are two, Taylor Slough and Shark River Slough.

You walk into the trees. You lose your balance and grab hold of a tree trunk to stop yourself from falling over. You get sticky tree sap on your fingers and wipe it on your pants. You don't give the sap a second thought. Until it starts to hurt. And then the pain gets worse.

These are poisonwood trees, and touching them can give people a nasty allergic reaction. The sap is especially irritating, as you've just found out. You use some of your precious drinking water to rinse your blistered skin. Then you cover it with a strip torn from a clean T-shirt you find in your backpack, and hope for the best.

You turn and try to find a way out of here.

Go to page 16.

Poisonwood

- Poisonwood is one of several poisonous plants native to the Everglades. Others that cause a similar reaction in humans are poison ivy, poison oak, and poison sumac.
- All of these plants contain oil called urushiol, which can cause a skin rash. Any part of the plant can cause the rash.
- A rash can even be caused indirectly, by touching something (clothing, for example), that's been in contact with the plant. Smoke from burning poisonwood can irritate people's lungs if it's inhaled. Even rainwater dripping from the leaves of a poisonwood tree can cause a rash.
- Usually it takes a few hours for the effects of poisonwood to be felt, but the effects of its sap can occur very quickly.
- Poisonwood produces fruit that's poisonous to people, but it's a favorite food of some birds and animals, including the rare white-crowned pigeon.

You find a tree to hide behind, make yourself comfortable, and wait. Just when you're thinking of giving up, you hear rustling in the undergrowth. Cautiously, a large tawny-colored cat stalks towards the dead animal. You shiver with fear—is it a panther? Maybe you've just made a big mistake.

But when you look more closely, you realize this animal is much too small to be a panther. It's more like a very large and fluffy pet cat. It's actually a bobcat, which feasts on the dead rabbit hungrily. After a while, it slinks back into the depths of the forest.

Go to page 66.

Florida Bobcat

- Bobcats live all over Florida—even in city suburbs. They range across the various Everglades habitats, and they are good swimmers.
- Like panthers, bobcats are tawny colored, but with black spots and stripes, and their ears have black tufts. They're much smaller than panthers, and on average are about twice the size of a domestic cat.
- Bobcats get their name from their short tails or "bobs."
- Bobcats aren't fussy eaters and will prey on small mammals, carrion (animals that are already dead), birds, and even insects.

You can't see very well, but you put your hand into a likely-looking hole in the rock. You feel a sharp sting and pull out your hand. To your horror, there's a snake attached to it! You shake your hand, panicking, and eventually the snake lets go and slithers back down into the hole.

The snake was bright red, yellow, and black. You know from your tour book that there's a venomous snake that looks a lot like it. But you also know there's a very similar snake that's completely harmless. You just can't remember how to tell the difference. After a moment or two, you start to feel better. The bite was no more painful than getting a needle from the doctor, and there's hardly any swelling. The snake must have been the harmless kind.

Unfortunately, you're wrong. Although there's no pain or swelling at the moment, without antivenom the snake's toxins start to work. Several hours later, you feel light-headed, your vision is blurred, and eventually you have to sit down. Soon you're unable to move, and it's not long before your heart and lungs stop working.

The end.

Eastern Coral Snake

- As a general rule, never put your hand into a dark cave or rock crevice if you can't see what's in there. A variety of dangerous creatures could be lurking unseen.
- Eastern coral snakes are found in the southeastern United States and northern Mexico. They are highly venomous.
- These snakes are brightly colored, with bands of red and black separated by thinner bands of yellow.
- The scarlet kingsnake looks very similar, but it isn't dangerous to people. You can tell which is which by looking at the colored bands—if red and yellow bands are next to one another, it's an eastern coral snake. If not, it's a scarlet kingsnake. There is a rhyme that helps people remember the difference: "Red and yellow kill a fellow, red and black friend of Jack."
- Eastern coral snakes aren't aggressive, and only bite if they're stepped on or touched. Their venom isn't easily injected, and there is an antivenom available. There have been no reported deaths from the bite of an eastern coral snake for nearly 50 years.

The pine trees are on higher ground, and it's a relief not to be wading through murky water. It's not as dark and gloomy here as in the cypress forest, because the trees are much further apart.

You had a very early start this morning, and you're feeling tired. Maybe you should have a rest?

If you decide to keep walking, go to page 24.

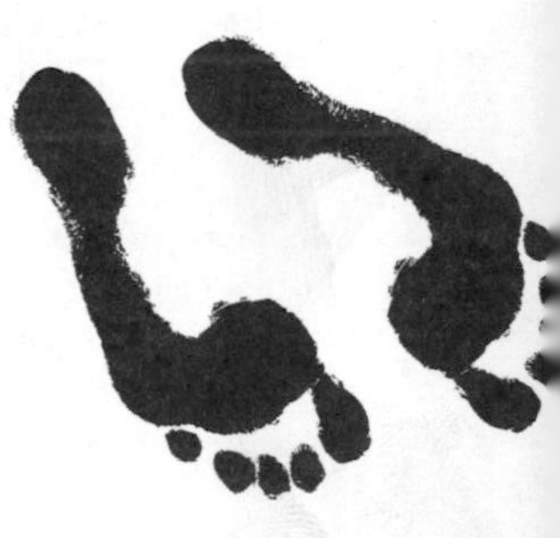

Everglades Pine Rockland Habitat

- As its name suggests, the trees in pine rocklands grow on rocky (limestone) ground.
- The pine trees are slash pines, and most of the lower-growing plants are a type of palm called saw palmetto.
- This habitat needs fire to survive. Lightning strikes cause natural fires that make it impossible for other trees to thrive here. The slash pines are protected by their thick bark, which means they can survive a fire. If there were no fires, the pine rocklands would be taken over by other plants. The Everglades National Park rangers sometimes set their own fires in the pinelands to give nature a helping hand.
- Pine rocklands in the Everglades can be difficult to walk in because the limestone rock can be sharp underfoot. It can also be dangerous, because of large holes or caves in the limestone, which aren't always visible.

The rattling sound is louder now, and suddenly a horrible thought occurs to you, sending shivers down your spine. What if it's a rattlesnake?

You gulp, and look at the ground. Sure enough, there's a snake coiled in front of you. It's less than 1.5 feet (0.5 m) away, shaking its tail to make the rattling noise. Its black tongue flits in and out, tasting the air.

If you decide to back away carefully, go to page 80.

If you decide to stay where you are until the snake backs off, go to page 52.

You make your way towards the pine forest, swishing your stick in front of you as you walk.

You jump as a snake darts past you, disturbed by the stick. In the distance you hear a bellowing sound. You think it's probably an alligator. A cold shiver runs down your back. You wade through the flooded ground as fast as the tearing sawgrass will let you.

Go to page 46.

As you wade through the flooded grassland, you realize that deciding to get out of it as quickly as possible is definitely a good idea. The grass (actually it's a type of sedge) is vicious stuff, ripping at your clothes and skin as you move.

You're also surrounded by clouds of biting insects. You can't wait to get to dry land.

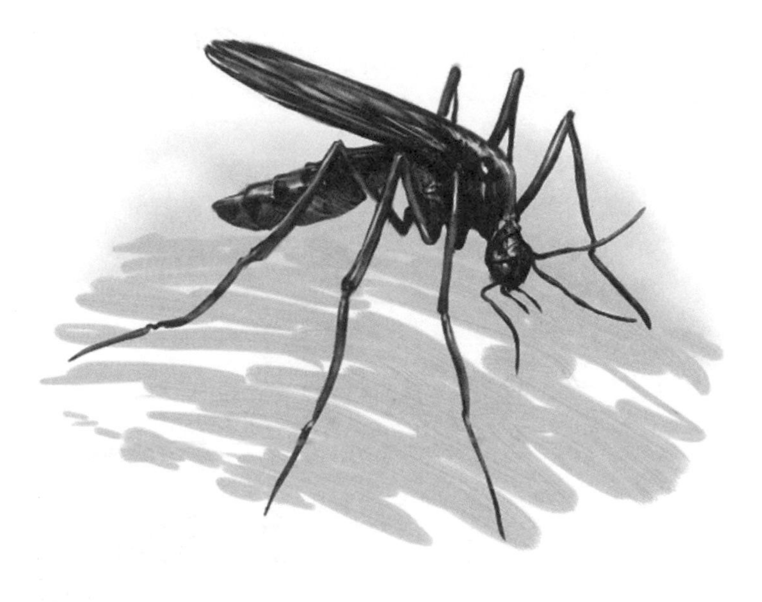

Go to page 46.

Everglades Mosquitoes

- Summertime in the Everglades, which is also the wet season, brings thick clouds of biting mosquitoes. In the winter, from around December to March, there aren't as many mosquitoes, because there is less water for them to lay their eggs in. But at the height of summer, they can be more than a nuisance, especially if you have an allergic reaction to their bites.

- Male mosquitoes feed on nectar in plants. Only females bite mammals, because they need the nutrients from the blood to produce their eggs.

- The mosquitoes here are the same type that cause the disease called malaria. When it bites, the mosquito passes on tiny parasites that cause the disease to mammals. Malaria kills hundreds of thousands of people every year, mainly in Africa. Malaria was common in the United States until the 1950s, when it was almost completely wiped out. Cases of malaria in the United States are very rare now.

- Unfortunately, mosquitoes aren't the only kind of biting insect found in the Everglades. You might also be feasted on by many other types of biting fly, including horse flies and deer flies.

The snake is rattling its tail because it feels threatened and is warning you to back off. When you don't, it strikes, and bites you on the lower leg.

The snake is a venomous eastern diamondback rattlesnake, and its bite is intensely painful. You drop to the ground, clutching your leg. Soon your whole body is in pain, and you start to feel very weak. Eventually, you have a heart attack and die.

The end.

Eastern Diamondback Rattlesnakes

- Eastern diamondback rattlesnakes are found in the southeastern United States. They're the largest venomous snake in North America, reaching up to 8.2 feet (2.5 m) long.
- The snake's skin is diamond-patterned in muted brown, black, and yellow, which camouflages it well.
- Like the cottonmouth (see page 23), rattlesnakes are pit vipers, which means they use heat-sensitive pits above their nostrils to sense the presence of prey.
- They can inject a lot of venom into their prey using their long fangs. They eat small mammals and birds.
- The snakes have a reputation for aggression, but in fact they only bite in self-defense. Their bites are rarely fatal to people because there's an antivenom available.
- The dusky pygmy rattlesnake is also found in the Everglades and is also venomous.

You trudge over the swampy ground. The sky above the treetops is cloudy, and it's dark here in the forest. Ahead of you it looks even gloomier. The cypress trees have given way to smaller trees thick with glossy, dark green leaves.

Maybe it's time to find a way out of the forest after all?

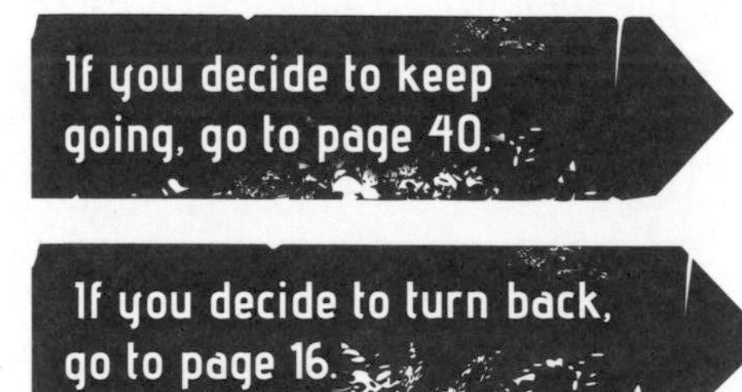

Some of the snakes in this flooded forest are deadly. You were right to turn back, especially since snakes often like to bask on the cypress knees you were using as hand-holds.

Through the trees, you think it looks lighter. Maybe you're getting close to the edge of the forest?

Go to page 38.

You're panicking as you dash through the pine trees, slipping on the sharp rock. You're no match for the speed and agility of the panther. Even though you're (very unwisely) running away from it, just like a prey animal would, the panther isn't chasing you.

Mountain lions (also known as cougars), which are the same species as Florida panthers, do sometimes attack people. But, luckily for you, there are no recorded attacks on humans by Florida panthers.

After a few minutes you stop running, completely out of breath, with your heart pounding wildly. You look around for the panther, but it's nowhere to be seen. You realize you've been very stupid to run away from a large, fast predator. You carry on walking through the pines and palmetto, keeping an eye out for the panther as you go.

Go to page 76.

Florida Panther

- Florida panthers are part of the same species as pumas (also known as cougars, mountain lions, and catamounts). They can measure up to about 6.6 feet (2 m) long, and weigh more than 154 pounds (70 kg).

- Panthers prey on deer, raccoons, other small mammals, and sometimes even alligators.

- As well as in the Everglades, Florida panthers are also found in Florida's other national parks: the Big Cypress National Preserve, and the Florida Panther Wildlife Refuge. This is only about 5% of the area that they used to roam in the past.

- These beautiful animals are rare. There are fewer than 100 Florida panthers left in the wild. In the past, they were hunted because they were seen as a threat to farm animals and people. Now their biggest threat is their shrinking territory. Their habitat has become smaller as towns and cities have grown.

- Florida Panthers are shy, and it's rare to see one. So you've actually been very lucky to spot one—although it probably didn't feel that way at the time!

You stumble as the rock under your feet gives way, making a nasty gash on your ankle. You wince, mop up the blood, and carry on. You use your stick to test the ground in front of you as you walk.

The pine rocklands can be a very dangerous place to walk because of the holes in the limestone. Even though you're testing the ground with your stick, your right foot catches the edge of a large hole in the rock underneath you. More rock gives way, and you plummet into a sinkhole, smashing your head and badly gashing your arms and legs on the sharp rock. Your injuries mean you don't make it.

The end.

Sinkholes

- The rock here is limestone, which absorbs water and is fairly soft and crumbly compared to other kinds of rock. These Everglades pine forests are dotted with sinkholes. Here in the pine rocklands, there's very little soil covering the rock.

- Solution holes are a type of sinkhole. They form over a long period of time, as rainwater mixed with acid from decaying leaves gradually eats away at the limestone. Sinkholes can also be caused when the ground subsides over time, or collapses suddenly, often due to changes in water levels.

- Sinkholes can also form in cypress forests (see page 13), and often become filled with water during the rainy season, or sometimes for most of the year, depending on whether they form on high or low ground.

- Florida has more sinkholes than any other state, because of its limestone base.

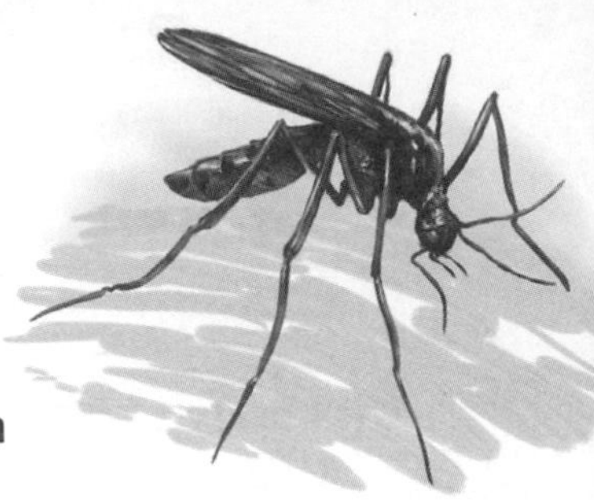

The sawgrass has scratched nasty wounds in your legs, and some of your mosquito bites have become infected. You swat another bug away as you wade wearily through the marsh.

There are mangroves in the distance. You wonder what your chances are of finding anybody canoeing there. It looks quite far away.

The flooded sawgrass is full of strange sounds. Birds call and shriek, and there are weird grunts, which might be made by the pig frogs you've heard about. Occasionally there is a bellowing sound, which you think must be made by alligators.

You are miserable, hot, completely exhausted, and terrified. After a while, you run out of water.

Your only hope now is rescue. Sadly, it doesn't arrive. You sink to your knees and pass out, drowning in the flooded prairie.

The end.

Your encounter with the crocodile has left you feeling shaken. What other creatures are waiting in Florida Bay?

But then you hear something that cheers you up—the sound of a motor! You scan the horizon, and when you spot the boat you very nearly capsize the canoe in your excitement. You start paddling toward it furiously.

Go to page 114.

You nod off into a fitful sleep. As you doze, something crawls out of the cobwebs in the palmetto and on to your face . . .

You wake up with a start and brush a small spider off your nose. As you do so it bites you twice, once on your cheek and then again on your hand.

You have been very unlucky. The spider is a black widow. At first, you're not even sure the spider has bitten you at all. You get up and start walking through the pine forest, but after fifteen minutes or so your face and hand start to ache. Soon you're feeling weak and sick. You slump to the ground, vomiting and in pain. It's not a pleasant way to go..

The end.

Black Widow Spiders

- Black widow spiders got their name because female spiders sometimes kill and eat the males after they've mated. They are fairly small spiders, only about 1.6 inches (4 cm) long, and they are black with a distinctive red mark on their abdomen. They're found all over North America.
- There are different kinds of widow spiders. In Florida, you will also find red widow. Australia's redback spider is a relative of the black widow.
- Widow spiders build a messy-looking web, and wait in a corner of it for their insect prey to become entangled.
- Black widows have powerful venom that has been known to kill people. However, bites are rare, because the spiders aren't usually aggressive.

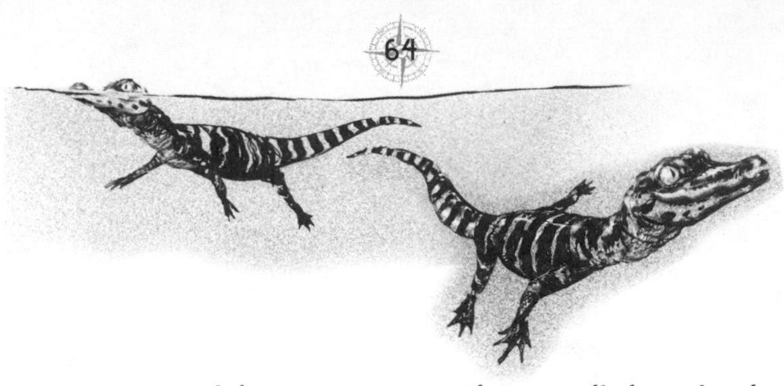

You were right to get away. The cute little animals were baby alligators, and their not-so-cute mother wasn't far away.

The wind is getting stronger as you struggle along through the mangroves in waist-deep murky water. The temperature has dropped, though it's still warm. However, it won't be long now until night falls, so you need to find somewhere to sleep.

A flash of blue catches your eye amongst the mangroves and you go to take a closer look. It's a canoe, entangled in the mangroves! After a lot of pushing and shoving, you manage to get it out. The boat is watertight. You're in luck! You use some rope you find in the bottom of the canoe to tie it securely to the mangroves, and climb in to spend the night there.

The wind is howling now, and it starts to rain. You hunker down, protected by the canoe and the mangroves from the worst of the wind and the rain. The storm rages for most of the night so you don't get much sleep. But as dawn breaks, the wind starts to die down.

You hope you won't have to spend another night in the wilderness.

Hurricanes and Tropical Storms

- Hurricanes are extreme tropical storms, with wind speeds of 73 miles (118 km) per hour or more. They're caused by warm air rising quickly, then being pushed aside as it cools, making it spin.
- Hurricane season in Florida lasts from June to November. Late August to October is the worst period.
- Hurricanes are given names. If a hurricane does a lot of damage, that name is never used again.
- More hurricanes hit Florida than any other US state. The Labor Day hurricane of 1935 was the most powerful ever to hit the United States, and killed more than 400 people in the Florida Keys. Hurricane Donna, in 1960, and Hurricane Andrew, in 1992, were two more of the most destructive hurricanes ever to hit Florida. But they weren't the most deadly.
- Florida's most deadly hurricane happened in 1928, when 2,000 people were washed away after a dike around Lake Okeechobee gave way.
- Hurricanes, typhoons, and cyclones are all the same type of storm, but the name that is used depends on where the storm hits. In the Atlantic and northeast Pacific Ocean it's a hurricane; in the northwest Pacific Ocean it's a typhoon; and in the South Pacific and Indian Ocean it's a cyclone.

You catch sight of something brightly colored on a tree trunk and go to take a closer look. It's a large snail, with the most beautiful shell you've ever seen. It has thin bands of bright yellow, orange, and gray spiraling around it. You notice that there are more snails on the tree.

Despite the fact that you're lost, you decide you have to take some photos. You get out your camera and snap some pictures of the amazing snails—they look as though they're made of porcelain. As you're putting the camera back into your backpack you drop it. You look on the forest floor, but can't see it anywhere.

The camera wasn't expensive, but it does have lots of pictures on it that you don't want to lose. Should you look for it? There are small holes in the rock. It probably dropped into one of them.

If you decide to search for your camera, go to page 44.

If you decide to forget about it, go to page 81.

Tree Snails

- The snails are Florida tree snails, which are native only to Florida and some of the islands in the Caribbean.
- They're quite big, up to about 2.8 inches (7 cm) long, with a tall, cone-shaped shell. The shells are often brightly colored, with stripes or other patterns.
- More than 50 color variations evolved within Florida, some of them restricted to a single small area.
- However, the beautiful shells were the snails' downfall, and in the early 20th century thousands of them were taken away by collectors.
- Some greedy collectors deliberately set fire to trees in order to wipe out snails of a particular type, so that the shells they had collected would be rarer and more expensive. Some types of tree snail died out completely as a result.

The panther continues to stare at you, but it doesn't move toward you. Eventually, it slinks off into the undergrowth. You stay where you are, peering into the forest, until you're sure it's gone.

You feel painful nips on your ankles, and look down to discover dozens of ants crawling all over your feet! You were so worried about the panther that you hadn't noticed them. You brush them off, rubbing the bites, which have formed tiny blisters.

Go to page 76.

Fire Ants

- These ants are fire ants, which have invaded the United States from South America and are very common in Florida.

- They are reddish-brown in color, and only about 0.1 inches (3 mm) long.

- Fire ants are famous for their painful stings, which feel like tiny burns. The stings form pustules on the skin, which can be extremely itchy for several days.

- The stings can become infected (especially if they're scratched), and ideally they should be thoroughly washed as soon as possible. Otherwise the ants aren't dangerous to people, unless you happen to be one of the few people who are allergic to their stings.

You wade through the flooded grassland as quickly as you can, keeping a wary eye out for alligators and snakes.

Soon you arrive at the forested higher ground. Which way should you go? Into the center of the forest? Or should you stick to the forest edge?

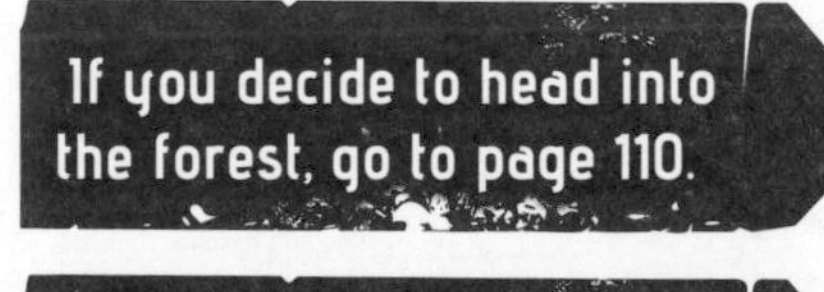
If you decide to head into the forest, go to page 110.

If you decide to keep to the edge, go to page 106.

Hardwood Hammock Habitat

- In the Everglades, higher ground where hardwood trees grow are known as "hammocks."
- Tropical hardwood trees such as mahogany grow on the dry higher ground. They grow quite close together, so it's shady and cool where they are found.
- There are many of different plant species here, including rare orchids. Trees with red, flaky bark are gumbo limbo trees.
- Native Americans who lived in the Everglades made their homes in hardwood hammocks, because they're more hospitable to people than other Everglades habitats.
- Watch out for solution holes, which are holes in the rock (see page 59), which might be filled with water, or even harbor an alligator.

You paddle quickly but carefully away from the crocodile. In fact, American crocodiles aren't actually considered dangerous to people. They're not aggressive, and there's only ever been one recorded attack on a person.

A dark shape catches your eye. For a moment, you freeze in terror. Could it be a shark's fin? You know there are dangerous sharks in Florida Bay. Before you can panic any further, the unmistakable shape of a dolphin's back curves above the waves. You let out a long sigh of relief. More dolphins appear, jumping and splashing around your canoe.

These beautiful creatures seem interested in you. Maybe you should take this once-in-a-lifetime opportunity to get out of the boat and swim with the dolphins? It's even more tempting as you realize you could wash the horrible sticky mud off you at the same time.

If you decide to swim with the dolphins, go to page 84.

If you decide to stay in your canoe, go to page 34.

Bottlenose Dolphins

- The dolphins in Florida Bay are bottlenose dolphins, which are found in warmer seas all over the world.
- They're usually seen in groups of between two and fifteen animals, but out at sea hundreds of them might group together.
- Bottlenose dolphins can measure up to about 13 feet (4 m) long, and weigh about 1,102 pounds (500 kg).
- They're famous for their watery acrobatics, and can jump up to 16.4 feet (5 m) out of the water.
- Dolphins find their fishy prey using echolocation, which means they make clicking sounds and listen to the echoes as the sound bounces back to them. They communicate with one another using squeaks and whistles.
- Dolphins have different methods of catching prey, including "fish whacking," where they knock fish out of the water using their tails!

Suddenly you're in the middle of one of your worst nightmares: you've walked straight into a huge spider's web! The cobweb clings to your face and shoulders. You shut your eyes tight and desperately claw the web off you—when part of it moves! You open your eyes to see a large spider with a long body squirming in the web, right on your face!

You scream as you brush the web and the spider off you. The creature scuttles off into the leaves on the forest floor. You hope the spider hasn't bitten you, but if it has, you hope it isn't venomous.

After that horrible experience, maybe you should get out of this forest?

If you decide to carry on as you are, go to page 107.

If you decide to find a way out of the forest, go to page 77.

Golden Silk Spider

- There are many different kinds of orb spider in the Everglades. The one you've just met is a golden silk spider (named after the color of its web), also known as a banana spider.
- Golden silk spiders are quite large, and they have long bodies. Including their bodies and legs, they're typically a bit bigger than the palm of your hand. The larger ones are females, and the males are much smaller.
- You'll be relieved to know that these spiders aren't dangerous—unless you're an insect. Their bites can become swollen and painful, though.
- The spiders weave large, geometric webs stretched between trees to catch their prey. A golden silk spider's web might be as long as 6.6 feet (2 m) across.

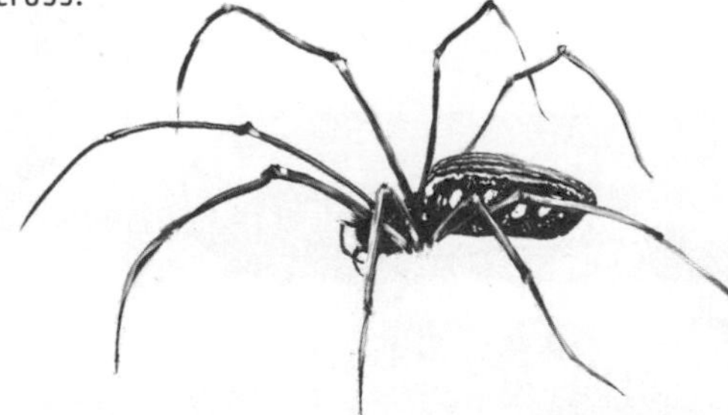

You stumble, and notice that the ground here is full of potholes. They don't seem very deep, but you need to be careful that you don't twist your ankle.

Maybe it would be better to find a way out of this pine forest? On the other hand, at least it's dry here.

If you decide to find a way out of the pines, go to page 90.

If you decide to keep going, go to page 93.

The ground slopes downward and you walk downhill, hoping that this will lead you out of the hardwood hammock and into fresher air.

Perhaps if you make it to the mangroves, where your group was going to go canoeing, you'll find other tourists.

Go to page 104.

You take a small bite. You're pretty sure the fruit can't be poisonous, because it tastes just as good as it smells. You're certain that poisonous plants usually taste bitter—it's common sense, after all. Satisfied with your reasoning, you eat the whole fruit.

But you have made a huge mistake. This is a manchineel, a very poisonous fruit. It's not long before your lips start to tingle, and a burning, peppery sensation begins inside your mouth. Soon your whole mouth and throat is swollen. You slump to the ground, struggling to breathe. In your weakened state, and without medical attention, you don't last long.

The end.

Manchineel

- The name of this tree comes from the Spanish *manzanilla de la muerte*, which means little apple of death. The fruit are also known as beach apples.
- It's found in the Everglades and also in Central America and the Caribbean.
- All of the manchineel plant is poisonous. The sap causes blistering and burns if it's touched, and if you stand underneath a manchineel tree while it's raining, the toxins on the leaves can give you a nasty rash, and even blisters. If the tree is burned, the smoke can injure people's eyes and cause lung problems.
- Although it's known to be poisonous, there are no recorded deaths from eating the fruit of the manchineel.

You back away, retracing your steps, and the noise stops. It was a very good idea to move as the sound was made by an eastern diamondback rattlesnake, which can be deadly (see page 53 to find out more).

You carry on, keeping an eye out for danger.

Go to page 102.

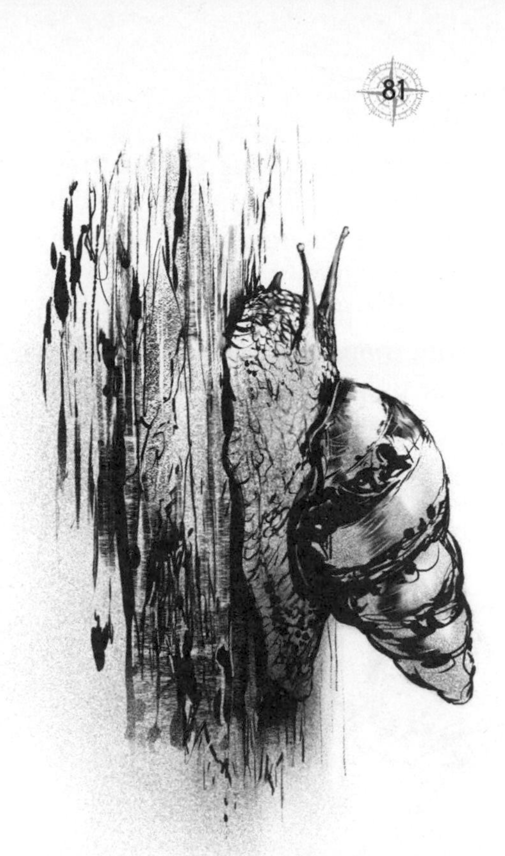

You peer at the holes in the rock. Anything could be lurking in there: snakes, spiders, scorpions...you shudder. It's a shame about the camera, but you're not risking putting your hand in there.

You carry on through the forest, and spot more colorful tree snails. It's a pity you won't have any photos to remember them by.

Go to page 74.

You should have been more concerned about those cute little swimming lizards. They're actually baby alligators. Even though alligators are known for being very dangerous creatures, they make very caring mothers. And the mother of these babies is 9.8 feet (3 m) long, weighs more than 550 pounds (250 kg), and is lurking just out of sight beneath the surface of the water.

The baby alligators cry out in distress as you come close to them. The mother alligator lunges out of the water ferociously, snapping her huge jaws around you and taking you completely by surprise. It's all over in a matter of seconds.

Alligator Babies

- American alligators mate in the spring, and this is the time that male alligators are most likely to be aggressive. They also bellow more, to declare their territory and to attract female alligators.
- Alligators lay their eggs in nests made from vegetation, usually in June or July. The temperature of the nest determines whether the baby alligators will be male or female.
- The baby alligators hatch out around two months later. They have yellow stripes and measure between 7.9 and 11.8 inches (20 and 30 cm).
- The mother alligator helps her babies to the water by carrying them in her mouth. She continues to protect her young for about a year.
- Find out more about American alligators on page 27.

The sun slips out from behind a cloud as you climb out of the canoe, and carefully place the paddle in the bottom of the boat. The water is shallow and warm, and it feels wonderful, soothing your bites and washing off the mud.

You look around for the dolphins, and sure enough two of them come over to investigate. They move so fast that you have no chance of keeping up with them, but they come back to you again and again, whistling and squeaking as they pass you. Then they're gone. You look for their sleek dark shapes in the water, but the dolphins have disappeared.

Unfortunately, the dolphins aren't the only large creatures swimming in Florida Bay. There are sharks here too, and one of them, an aggressive bull shark, is alerted to your presence as you splash back to the canoe. It lunges at you and takes a savage bite, killing you instantly.

The end.

Bull Shark

- Bull sharks are some of the world's most dangerous sharks. Along with great white sharks and tiger sharks, they're one of the three sharks that are most likely to attack people. They like warm, shallow water, where people tend to swim, and they are aggressive.
- Bull sharks measure up to about 11.5 feet (3.5 m) long, and can weigh up to about 551.2 pounds (250 kg).
- These sharks can live in freshwater as well as seawater, and can be found in rivers hundreds of miles from the sea.

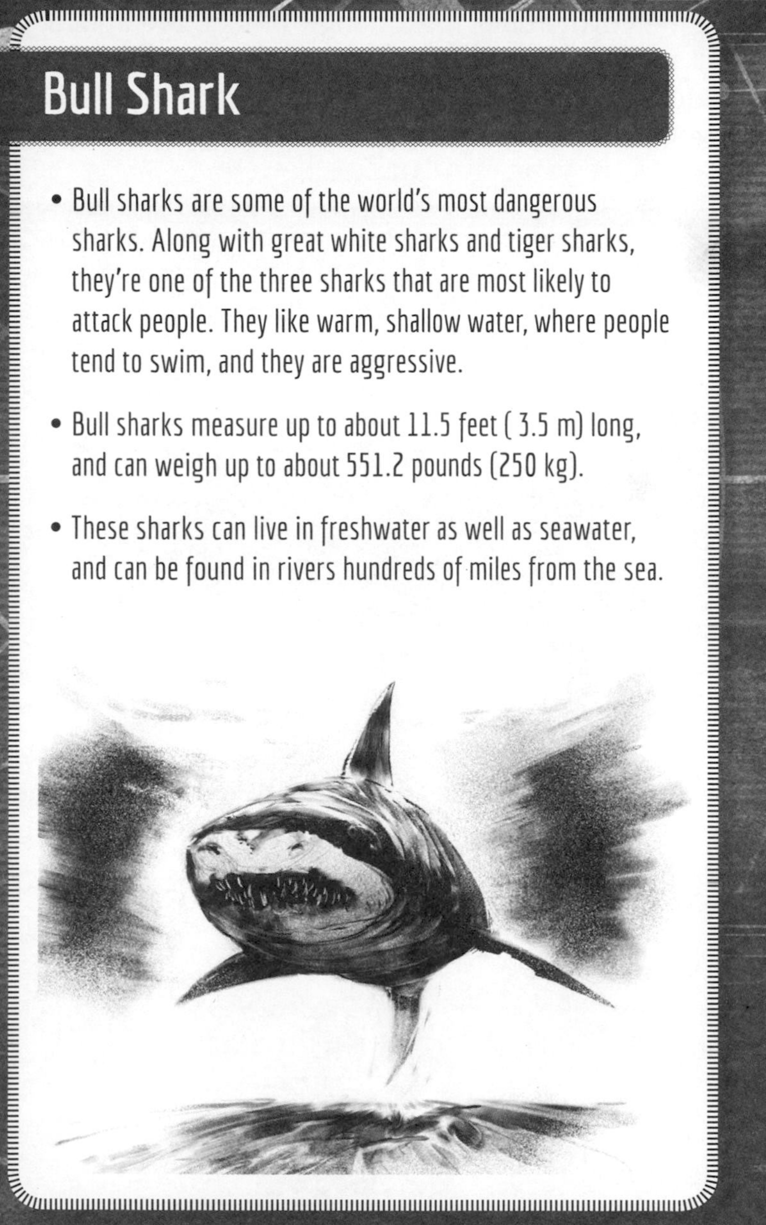

The coyote does look mangy. In fact, the animal is very sick—it has rabies. This makes it aggressive and unpredictable, unlike most coyotes, which wouldn't usually attack a human being.

The coyote runs at you, knocks you to the ground, and bites your throat savagely. If the terrible attack hadn't already killed you, you would have contracted the terrible disease rabies, which would be fatal without urgent treatment.

The end.

Coyotes

- Coyotes are close relatives of the gray wolf, and are sometimes called prairie wolves or brush wolves. They're smaller and much more widespread throughout North America.
- Coyotes measure up to about 51 inches (130 cm) from nose to tail, and weigh up to about 55 pounds (25 kg).
- Coyotes are adaptable animals: they will eat small mammals, fish, frogs, snakes, insects, fruit, and carrion. Some have adapted to live in big cities.
- The animals live in family groups. They form packs in the autumn and winter to make hunting more effective.
- They should be considered dangerous. There are many reports of coyote attacks on people, and some of the animals have been found to be carrying rabies.

You were right not to eat the fruit—it was poisonous manchineel (see page 79). It's never wise to eat anything you find unless you know for sure that it's safe, and even then you should check with a responsible adult.

As you wade through the mangroves, you begin to wonder whether this was such a good idea. Your group planned to canoe here, but the mangrove swamp is vast and they're long gone by now anyway. But you decide to keep going. If you can get to Florida Bay there are bound to be boats that can rescue you.

As you continue walking you spot a cute little creature. It looks like a swimming lizard with yellow stripes, similar to a mini alligator. Another one is following close behind it. They're making sweet little mewing noises. You wonder if they could be dangerous.

If you decide to stay away from the little lizards, go to page 64.

If you're not bothered by them, go to page 82.

From the corner of your eye, you catch a glimpse of a tawny-colored shape moving swiftly through the pine trees. You blink and look hard. You're unbelievably lucky, because you've just spotted a rare Florida panther. It's probably stalking the white-tailed deer you just saw.

Go to page 108.

After fifteen minutes or so of very careful walking, you come to the edge of the pine forest. Beyond the trees, you hear a distant splash and a gurgling hiss and you shudder. It's probably an alligator. There is still no sign whatsoever of other people. It's hard to believe this is 21st-century America. It looks more like a desolate swamp in the time of the dinosaurs.

You come to a sudden stop, your heart in your mouth. Not too far away from you stands an enormous bird. It looks as though it's flown in from prehistoric times. It has a vicious-looking beak, and it's looking out over the flooded grassland, standing very still. You back away. You recognize the bird as a heron, but you've never seen a giant one like this before, and who knows what it might do if it feels threatened? Your movement startles the bird into flight, and it soars into the sky.

Go to page 70.

Birds of the Everglades

Many people come to the Everglades just to see the different bird species that live there. More than 360 different species have been spotted in the Everglades, and some of them are very rare. Here are just a few of them:

- The heron you've just seen is a great blue heron, which can reach 55.1 inches (140 cm) tall. Tri-colored herons, great white herons (also known as great egrets), little blue herons, and little green herons can also be found here.

- Anhingas, water birds with long, thin necks, dive completely underwater to catch fish, which they impale with their sharp beaks.

- American bitterns have strange, gurgling cries, and you're more likely to hear one than see it. Their brown stripes camouflage them in the marsh grasses of the Everglades.

- Roseate spoonbills have beautiful pink feathers. They swing their spoon-shaped beaks backward and forward to filter food from the water.

- There are also many different kinds of birds of prey in the Everglades, such as great-horned owls, red-shouldered hawks, ospreys, and bald eagles. Vultures sometimes cause problems by ripping off the rubber trims from car windshield wipers!

You paddle onward, hoping to spot a boat that might come to your rescue.

You take your eyes off the horizon and spot something much closer. There's no mistaking what it is—a crocodile, and quite a big one. What should you do?

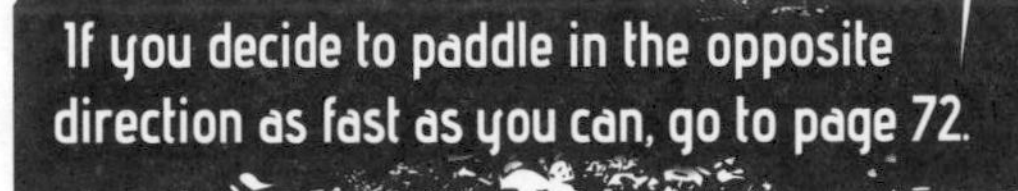

If you decide to paddle in the opposite direction as fast as you can, go to page 72.

If you decide to paddle past the crocodile calmly, go to page 94.

The rock here has a lot of holes in it. You're being very careful and testing the ground in front of you with your stick. Even so, you sometimes stumble as the rock crumbles and gives way under your weight.

Go to page 58.

The creature's sharp white teeth are revealed along its jaw, creating an evil smile, and as you approach it, you wonder if this was such a good idea after all. The creature looks longer than your canoe!

Lucky for you, American crocodiles aren't aggressive animals, unlike the saltwater crocodiles that live in Australia or the Nile crocodiles found in Africa, both of which kill people every year. As you paddle past the creature, it begins to move in the opposite direction, swimming gracefully away.

Go to page 61.

American Crocodile

- The Everglades is the only place on Earth where both alligators and crocodiles live. Crocodiles can live in the brackish (slightly salty) water of the mangroves, where alligators also live.
- Crocodiles in the Everglades can reach up to about 13.1 feet (4 m). American crocodiles in Central and South America can be much bigger—up to 19.7 feet (6 m) long.
- You can tell the difference between American alligators and American crocodiles by the shape of their snouts. Alligators' snouts are U-shaped, while crocodiles' are more V-shaped. American alligators are also much darker in color than crocodiles.
- American crocodiles might look meaner than the alligators, but they're not. Alligators are far more aggressive. It's almost unheard of for an American crocodile to attack people.
- American crocodiles are rare. In the past, they were hunted for their skins, or for wild animal shows. While the alligator population has improved since then, the number of crocodiles is still low.

It soon becomes obvious what the smell was. You spot a small black and white animal, with two white stripes running down its back and a bushy tail. It's a skunk! These animals are famous for their stinky spray.

The skunk is about 9.8 feet (3 m) away from you. You're just about to make your escape when it raises its tail and takes aim. Despite the distance, you're overpowered with one of the most disgusting smells you've ever encountered, as the skunk showers you with tiny droplets of foul-smelling liquid. You've heard about skunks and how badly they smell, but the stench is overpowering! You cover your nose and mouth with your hands, and back away from the animal as fast as you can.

You decide to head out of the hardwood forest and into some fresher air. You head for the mangroves.

Go to page 77.

Everglades Skunks

- The animal you've just encountered is a striped skunk, also known as a polecat. Its white stripes can vary so that some striped skunks' backs are completely white. The animals measure up to about 27.6 inches (70 cm) long, with bushy tails about 35 cm) long.
- The skunk uses its spray to ward off predators. Its scent glands can spray up to 14.8 feet (4.5 m) and the smell can be detected 1.6 miles (2.5 km) away!
- Striped skunks eat insects mostly, but also reptiles, small animals such as mice and frogs, fruit, other plant matter, and fungi.
- The animal's main predator is the great horned owl. It's immune to the skunk's terrible smell.
- The Eastern spotted skunk is a smaller animal, black with white spots and wavy stripes. It's just as smelly as the striped skunk, and can also spray up to 14.8 feet (4.5 m)—but you'll get a better warning, because it does a series of handstands before it releases its horrible whiff.
- If you ever need to get away from a skunk, remember that striped skunks can't climb trees, while eastern spotted skunks can.

This was the right direction to choose. You paddle out of the mangroves and into the shallow open sea of Florida Bay. In the distance, a pelican dives into the calm water.

The sun appears from behind a cloud. Apart from an ominous dark shape in the middle distance, the water looks blue and clear. There's a snorting noise as a whiskery nose surfaces and takes a breath. You've heard about these animals before and decide that it must be a manatee.

You know that manatees won't hurt you. Should you go and take a closer look?

If you decide to investigate, go to page 112.

If you decide not to, go to page 92.

Florida Bay Habitat

- Florida Bay, at the southern tip of Florida, is very shallow, only about 9.8 feet (3 m) deep. The freshwater flowing into it from the Everglades means that its salt content varies quite dramatically.

- Much of the seabed in Florida Bay is covered in plant life, including sea grass, a favorite food of the manatee. Corals and sponges also grow in the bay.

- Mangrove islands, dotted around the bay, are often nurseries for young fish and other sea creatures.

- Many different fish are found in Florida Bay, including barracuda, sharks, and rays. There are also marine mammals such as dolphins and manatees.

You paddle through the mangroves, struggling to negotiate twisted roots and branches. Unfortunately, you're not heading in the right direction to get to the sea. Even more unfortunately, there's an absolutely massive python lying half out of the water on one of the mangrove roots.

You don't see it until it's too late. The enormous snake grabs you by the shoulder, its sharp teeth digging in to hold you fast while it coils itself around you. These snakes kill their prey not by injecting venom, but by squeezing them so that they can no longer breathe. You struggle, but it's pointless.

The end.

Burmese Python

- The Burmese python has no business living in the United States at all. Burmese pythons are native to Southeast Asia, including Myanmar, which is also called Burma.
- Pythons are constricting snakes, which squeeze their prey to death rather than injecting it with venom.
- Starting in the 1980s, Burmese pythons were introduced to the Everglades. They probably escaped from, or were released into the wild by, people who had kept them as pets.
- They've thrived in their new home, and now there may be hundreds of thousands living in the Everglades.
- The pythons are having a devastating effect in the Everglades as they prey on the animals native to the area, including white-tailed deer, marsh rabbits, bobcats, other mammals, and even alligators!
- Burmese pythons can grow to 23 feet (7 m) long and weigh up to 198 pounds (90 kg). The largest one on record is 27 feet (8.23 m) long. They are good swimmers, and can stay underwater for half an hour without needing to breathe.

A movement among the tall pine trees catches your eye: it's a deer. You watch the beautiful animal for a moment, its white tail bobbing along through the trees.

Should you carry on walking in the same direction as the deer? Or do you worry that a predator might be after it?

If you carry on in the same direction as the deer, go to page 89.

If you decide to change direction, go to page 76.

White-tailed Deer

- White-tailed deer are medium-sized deer, and are the smallest that are found in North America. They're found from southern Canada all the way south to South America.
- The deer raise their fluffy white tails as an alarm signal to other deer if they sense a predator.
- In the Everglades, the deer have plenty of predators, including alligators, bobcats, coyotes, constricting snakes, and Florida panthers.
- White-tailed deer in Florida are generally smaller than white-tailed deer found elsewhere, as they don't need extra fat to protect them from the cold. They weigh about 110 pounds (50 kg).

As you walk you see less hardwood trees, and the interwoven trunks and roots of mangrove trees appear.

Soon, the weirdly shaped trees surround you. You're wading now, as the water reaches up over your knees. You keep a wary eye out for alligators and crocodiles, as you remember that the guide said both can live in these mangrove swamps. You call out, in case there are any canoeists around, but there's no reply.

Not all of the trees are mangroves. One of them bears a small fruit that looks just like an apple. You're very hungry and tired. Eating something might be just the thing to keep your spirits up.

If you decide to eat the fruit, go to page 78.

If you decide not to, go to page 88.

Mangrove Habitat

- Mangrove forests thrive around the southern coast of Florida, and Florida Bay is dotted with mangrove islands. Their twisted roots make a maze of waterways.
- There are three different species of mangrove in the Everglades: red, black, and white mangrove. The leaves of a black mangrove are often covered in salt, which has been expelled by the plant. Other salt-tolerant plants live in mangrove habitats, too.
- This habitat is home to animals including alligators, crocodiles, pythons, and water snakes.
- Leaves dropped into the water by mangroves grow a slimy layer of bacteria which produces tiny plants and fungi, and becomes the basis of the food chain.
- Mangrove forests protect the coastline from tropical storms and hurricanes.

In the undergrowth ahead of you there's a surprising sight: a dog. For a moment you think it must be someone's pet, and you call out in case the owners are close by. But the animal turns toward you, and you quickly realize that it's actually a mangy coyote.

You are sure that coyotes aren't dangerous, and this one looks a bit sick anyway. It doesn't seem to be moving normally, and its coat is falling out. You don't think it could possibly pose a threat to you.

Should you ignore the coyote, or go out of your way to avoid it?

If you decide to avoid the coyote, go to page 109.

If you decide to keep going, go to page 86.

A horrible musty smell hits your nostrils. Maybe there's an animal carcass rotting away somewhere. Or perhaps it's just really strong-smelling stagnant water or mud. Whatever it is, it's pretty disgusting.

First a huge spider on your face, and now this. Maybe the smell is a sign that you really should get out of this forest.

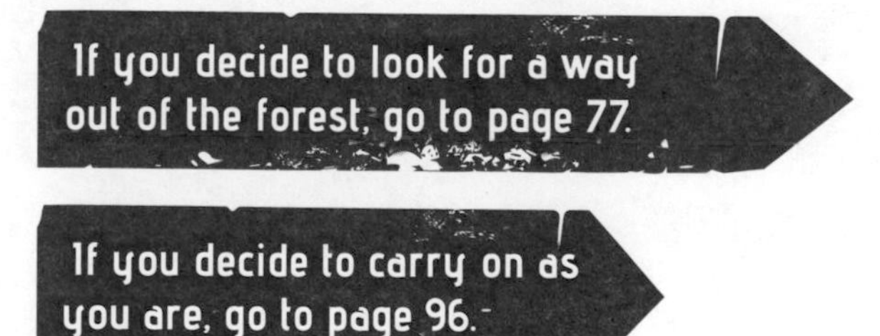

In your excitement at seeing the panther, you trip over a stone and crash noisily to the ground. You grab hold of a branch as you fall, and as you stand up and dust yourself off, you look in the direction of the panther and the deer. You can just about make out the white tail of the deer as it runs away through the trees. You can't see the panther, though.

Suddenly, you catch sight of the big cat and it's much closer than before. The animal isn't interested in the deer anymore. It's staring at you. What should you do?

If you decide to run away, go to page 56.

If you decide to back away, go to page 68.

You were right to get away from the coyote. Although they're not usually dangerous to people, that one looked as though it was sick. It might have had rabies.

You carry on through the forest, keeping an eye out for snakes, or anything else that might be dangerous. All you spot are a few lizards clinging to the red bark of gumbo limbo trees.

Go to page 74.

You haven't walked very far when you hear something rustling through the undergrowth—maybe you've disturbed something? As you walk on a bit further, you find the gory remains of what might have been a marsh rabbit.

Should you get away from here as soon as you can, or hide and find out what's made the kill? It's only a rabbit, after all, so it's probably not a very big predator.

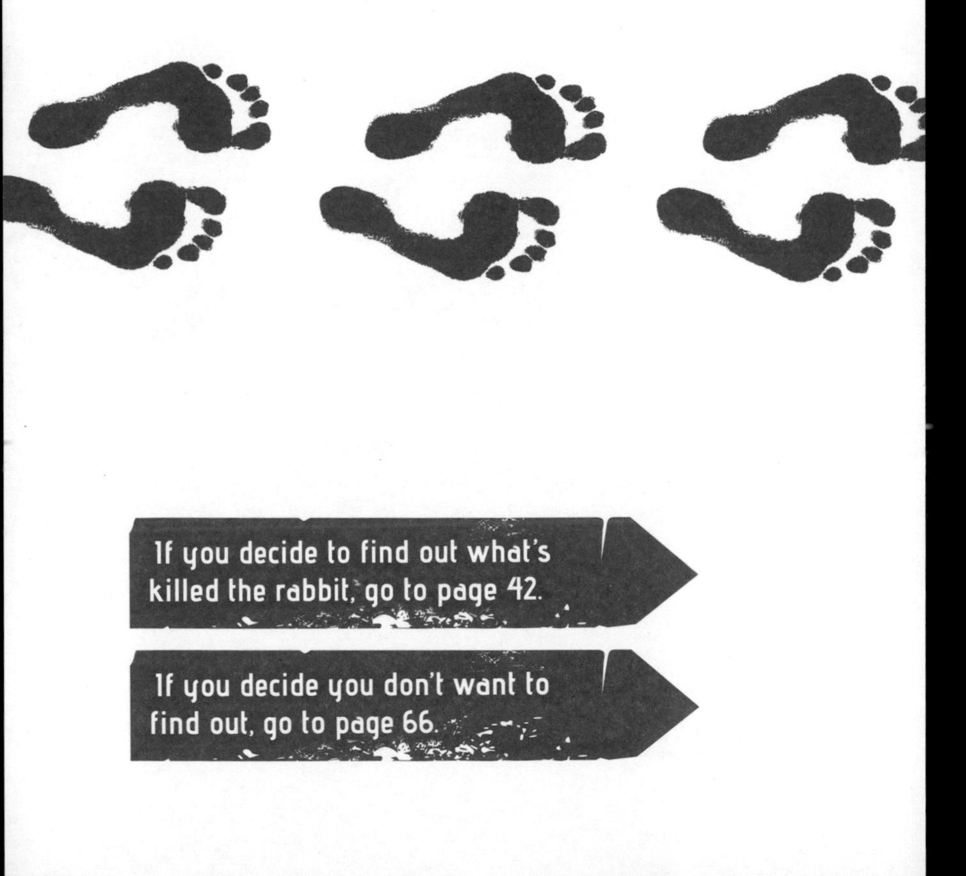

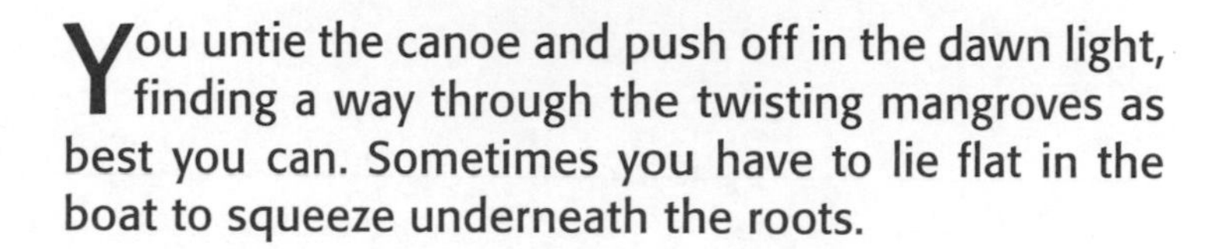

You untie the canoe and push off in the dawn light, finding a way through the twisting mangroves as best you can. Sometimes you have to lie flat in the boat to squeeze underneath the roots.

You come to a fork. There are two navigable ways through the mangroves: one is straight ahead of you, and the other is to your right. The sun comes out from behind a cloud to your left. You should be heading south in order to get out into Florida Bay and find a boat to rescue you. But which route will take you there?

If you take the route to your right, go to page 100.

If you paddle the route that's straight ahead of you, go to page 98.

You steer your canoe toward the manatees. These huge, gentle creatures are no threat to you, and tourists often snorkel with them. You watch the huge, gray manatees as they feed on the underwater sea grass, occasionally sticking their whiskered snouts out of the water to breathe. This was too good an opportunity to miss!

After watching the gentle creatures for a while, you come back to your senses and realize that there are more important things to worry about, such as finding rescue. You paddle off into the sea, still within sight of the coast, hoping to find a boat.

Go to page 92.

Manatees

- Manatees are also known as “sea cows” because, like cows, they are big, gentle, and eat grass (sea grass, anyway).
- They live in the coastal seas of the Caribbean and the Gulf of Mexico. There are two other species: one lives in the River Amazon, and the other along the coast and in the rivers of West Africa.
- Manatees can weigh up to 4,409 pounds (2,000 kg), and might eat up to 110 pounds (50 kg) of marine plants in a single day!
- Manatees used to be hunted for their meat and bones, but today they’re protected. The biggest threat to them is crashing into motor boats.

You can see two people on the boat now, and start waving frantically. The boat's motor is cut, and one of them calls out to you. When they realize your predicament, the couple on the boat pull up alongside your canoe in a matter of seconds.

Soon you're wrapped in a warm blanket aboard the motor boat. Your body is covered in cuts, bruises, and insect bites, and you are completely exhausted. The woman pours you a cup of hot chocolate from a flask before you head back to land, and you don't think you've ever tasted anything so delicious in your life.

Your adventure in the Everglades is over.

The end.

The People of Florida

Over thousands of years, different people have come to the Everglades, either to live or to explore. They include Native Americans, conquerors from Europe, settlers, and scientists. Today, nearly 20 million people live in Florida. The biggest built-up area is Miami and the area surrounding it, which is in southern Florida and has a population of 5.5 million.

Calusa People

From around three thousand years ago, the Calusa people were some of the first to live in Florida. They lived on the coast and along the rivers of southwest Florida, fishing and hunting for food. They built houses on stilts and used woven palmetto leaves for their roofs. Calusa buildings made from shells, as well as shell tools and jewelry, can still be found in Florida today. When the conquerors from Europe arrived, some of the Calusa people were sold into slavery and some died from the new diseases (such as smallpox) brought by the Europeans. By the late 1700s, hardly any Calusa people were left.

Invaders

The first European to set foot in Florida was Spanish explorer Ponce de Leon in 1513. He believed Florida was an island, and never realized that it was part of a huge continent. He named the land Florida (Spanish for "flowery land"), because of all the flowers he saw there when he first arrived. After his arrival, more Europeans came, and they kept coming. The area changed from being Spanish to British, and then finally American.

Seminole People

By the 1700s, as a result of more and more Europeans settling in the north of Florida, some Native American tribes, such as the Seminole and Miccosukee, decided to move into the south of Florida. But by the 1800s, the European settlers were trying to force them out of the South as well. The Seminole fought back, resulting in the "Seminole Wars." The third Seminole War ended in 1856, when the remaining Seminole people agreed to hand over two million acres of land to the settlers.

Draining the Everglades

Today, the Everglades is about a fifth of the size it once was. In the early 1900s, vast areas of Everglades wetlands were dredged and drained, and then used for crops. More people continued to settle there, and towns and cities grew. Mangrove swamps were cleared so that people had good sea views, and new canals and roads were built. Gradually, the Everglades shrank.

The animals of the Everglades had less space to live in, and many of them also had to contend with hunters. Beautiful Everglades birds were hunted for their feathers, alligators and crocodiles for their skins, and Florida panthers were killed because they were a danger to farm animals.

Today, organizations such as the Everglades Foundation are trying to preserve and restore the Everglades and its animals.

Endangered Everglades

Not surprisingly, many Everglades animals and plants are endangered. Here are just some of the threatened and endangered animals of the Everglades:

- American crocodile (see page 95)
- Eastern indigo snake
- Florida bonneted bat
- Florida leafwing butterfly
- Florida panther (see page 57)
- Key Largo cotton mouse
- Key Largo woodrat
- Manatee (see page 113)
- Red-cockaded woodpecker
- Snail kite
- Turtles, including the green sea turtle, hawksbill sea turtle, Kemp's ridley sea turtle, and leatherback sea turtle
- Wood stork
- White-crowned pigeon

True Tales

People really have ended up lost in the Everglades. Here are just a few of the terrifying tales that really happened.

In April 2013, the **Schreck family** was on holiday in Florida, taking a tour of the Everglades in an airboat borrowed from a friend. The boat became stuck in reeds, and the family of five, including three boys aged nine, seven, and three, couldn't move it. They were completely lost, and had to rely on their life jackets to keep them warm and dry during the cold, rainy night. Family members raised the alarm when the Schrecks didn't return home, and rescuers began the search for the family. The family was saved the following day, when rescuers heard their distress horns and whistles.

In 2007, **Carol Swingle** drove into the Everglades from her Miami home to take photos. On her way back to her car, and after a close encounter with an alligator, she took a wrong turn and soon realized she was hopelessly lost. She decided not to walk any further and wait for rescuers, since she couldn't be very far from the road. It turned out to be the right decision. Swingle was found after her son raised the alarm, but only after two days spent alone in the wilderness, wearing only shorts, a T-shirt, and flip-flops, and without any water, food, or insect-spray.

Jamey Mosch got lost in the Everglades in 2009, when he became separated from the rest of his hunting party. He wasn't found for four days, by which time he'd been stalked by a panther, badly bitten by mosquitoes, lost most of his clothes and equipment in a patch of thick mud, and had begun to hallucinate. He found a stream that was safe to drink from, where he also discovered a catfish that he ate raw. He also ate raw bullfrogs.

Glossary

antivenom a substance used to treat snake bites

bask lie in a sunny place, soaking up the sun's warmth

canopy the highest layer of branches in a forest

compensate make up for

dike a bank of earth built to protect an area from flooding

echolocation using the echoes of calls to figure out where objects are

fatal causing death

food chain the link between different living things that eat each other. Plants are eaten by plant-eating animals, which are eaten by meat-eating animals, which are eaten by bigger meat-eating animals.

gory covered in blood

hallucinate see things that are not really there

humid having a lot of moisture in the air

hunker crouch down and settle for a while

hydrated having enough water in your body

impale pierce with a sharp, pointed object

inhospitable uninviting, unfriendly, or difficult

mangrove swamps swampy coastal habitats where mangrove trees grow

mangy scruffy and ill-looking

navigable deep and wide enough to get a boat through

ominous indicating future misfortune or disaster

parasite an organism that lives in or on another organism, causing it harm

prairies large, flat grassland areas in North America

predicament difficult situation

primeval from the very earliest times on Earth

rabies a fatal disease passed on by the bites of infected animals

reclaimed land that was once under water, but has been drained

pustules infected blisters or spots

serrated having a notched or saw-like edge

sinkholes holes in the rock, formed when water dissolves the rock

sloughs deep river-like channels flowing through swampy grassland

stagnant not flowing, stale

tawny brownish-orange

terrain ground, what a particular area of land is like

toxins poisonous substances

venomous capable of injecting venom

waterline marks the highest level reached by water

Learning More

Arnosky, Jim. *The Pirates of Crocodile Swamp*. G.P. Putnam's Sons, 2009.

Long, Denise. *Survivor Kid: A Practical Guide to Wilderness Survival.* Chicago Review Press, 2011.

Lynch, Wayne. *Everglades (Our Wild World)*. Cooper Square Publishing, 2007.

Raffa, Edwina. *Escape to the Everglades*. Pineapple Press, 2013.

Tarshis, Lauren. *I Survived: True Stories*. Scholastic Inc., 2014.

Tillery, Reid. *Surviving the Wilds of Florida.* Collingwood Publications, 2005.

Websites

The Official Site of Everglades National Park
www.nps.gov/ever/index.htm

Information on Activities and Wildlife in the Florida Everglades
www.everglades-info.com

Everglades Swamp Safari
www.animalplanet.com/tv-shows/animal-planet-presents/videos/planets-best-everglades-swamp-safari/

What to Do When You're In A Wilderness Survival Situation (Equipped to Survive Foundation)
www.equipped.org/kidprimr.htm

List of Great Books About Survival (Indianapolis Public Library)
www.imcpl.org/kids/blog/?page_id=12516

Tips for How to Survive in Extreme Situations (Animal Planet)
www.animalplanet.com/tv-shows/i-shouldnt-be-alive/videos/survival-tips-videos.htm

Index

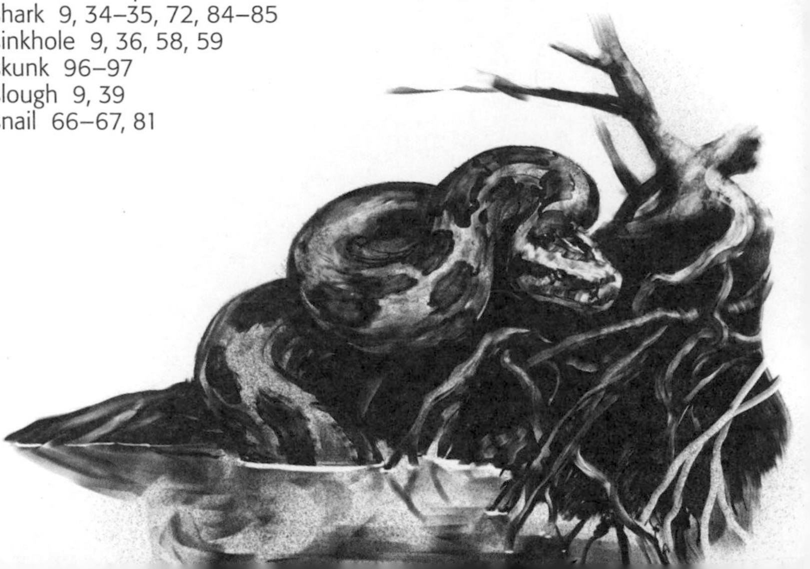